Dark Rites

Dark Rites

Iridescent Toad Publishing

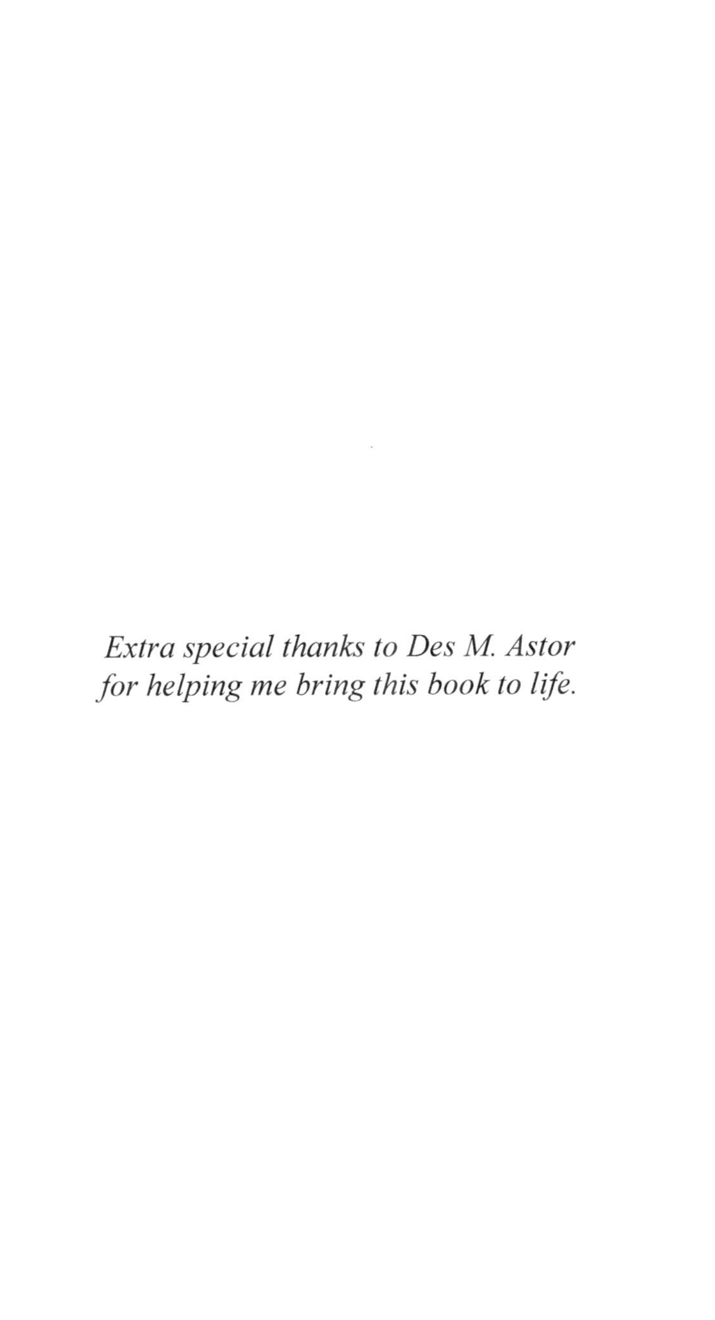

*Extra special thanks to Des M. Astor
for helping me bring this book to life.*

Chapter One

There it was again. The maddening clawing in the pit of her stomach, like a chained beast trying to rip free of its bindings. The pounding of her heart wasn't a big enough distraction, as was confirmed by the saliva pooling in her mouth and coating her lips.

Alana was hungry.

She couldn't deny her nature, but that didn't mean that she wanted to embrace it. On the contrary.

There on her knees in the dirt, the stars twinkling mockingly above, the moon almost seeming to laugh, she let out a guttural snarl. Was this corpse in front of her there due to her frenzy? She couldn't remember losing control. Blood dripped down her arm, causing her to quickly draw her tongue over her slightly tanned skin.

Tears began to crawl down her cheeks as her entire body shook. She retracted her tongue, bringing her hands up and burying her face into her palms. As the clouds gathered above to shed their rain, she sobbed, unable to handle the *urge*.

The weather began to clean the blood from her flesh, temporarily at least. After several minutes that felt like hours, Alana rose, rolling her shoulders back and drawing in a deep breath.

"I need to get ahold of myself and think," she muttered aloud to herself.

She wiped away the tears and blinked several times. She gazed about, taking in the scenery. She was in the forest at the edge of Temes, a town she'd grown used to over the last few centuries. The pine trees swayed in the storm's wind, their needles shuddering slightly from the patter of the rain. The scent of wood and smoke filled her senses; she was thankfully far enough from the town to avoid the scent of luscious blood. For now.

The matter of the corpse needed to be addressed, no doubt. Alana composed herself further, eventually looking it over. The pale of their flesh was littered with what looked like pinpricks, but

Alana knew better. *Vampire bites. Are they...
mine?*

She reached up, running a gentle finger over her
pristine canines, feline-like in nature. That
clawing urge, at times, caused her to lose control.
But she'd been keeping a hold on that for several
years, and the incidents had gone down. What
was going on *now,* then? Her lips morphed into
a scowl as she stared up to the thin clouds, as if
expecting them to provide an answer. The storm
was a small one, no doubt already preparing to
pass.

Even as that thought crossed her mind, the wisps
parted to reveal the moon, once more staring
down at her. Narrowing her eyes, Alana
continued to study the body, determining it was
that of a middle-aged man with fancy garb and
slicked-back dark hair. Perhaps he had been
visiting from the town several moons away, for
she didn't recognise him. How strange.

Bracing herself, Alana grabbed hold of his leg
and dragged him out of the clearing and deeper
into the woods. She proceeded to flex her claws,
digging into the dirt with them. They weren't
meant to be tools in this fashion, but she didn't
care. She was going to respect the dead, whether

or not she was the cause of this.

Her enhanced strength allowed her to proceed with ease, though it still took about an hour. The corpse was pushed into the shallow grave, and she took care to pack the dirt around it. As she searched for a stone to mark the grave properly, she tensed. The coppery scent of blood hit her nostrils, causing her to let out a guttural growl from the pit of her stomach.

Not now… not now…

The image of thick, crimson liquid – life-giving and wonderful, a taste beyond the most scrumptious of human dishes – made itself at home in her mind. She drew her tongue over her lips as the lust took her over for just a moment, the urge to snap and hunt down her prey gnawing at her incessantly.

No… no. It's wrong. I cannot. I'm not a monster.

Alana managed to call herself back, her head clearing as she flared her nostrils again. Although the scent of blood hit her, it wasn't that which provided the sharp pang of alarm. The musk of bat alerted her to a colony. But there was something else that stood out to her. As she looked to the sky again, she spotted the nocturnal creatures gathering above, flying about in a dance-like manner.

Her senses told her, however, that there was one not like the others. She narrowed her gaze, honing in on the culprit. *There...* These animals primarily fed on insects such as moths. One of them was covered in human blood though. Alana's eyes shifted to the corpse of the man, and that's when things clicked.

The blood on that bat belonged to him.

Her lips peeled upwards, forming her mouth into a scowl. Something out of the ordinary was going on here. Her hand twitched towards the silver knife in the sheath on her belt. She used it for only the direst of circumstances – namely, to defend the town against other vampires. She was fully aware of the irony, but the issues cropping up from her kind had been on the increase as of late.

A red gleam covered her before she too was a bat, flying in a crooked manner towards the colony. The shrill cries of the other bats disoriented her; it had been years since she'd taken this form. The wind whistled through her fur, the force fighting against the fleshy webbing of her wings.

She let out a shriek, tumbling off-course after not getting far off the ground at all. Within a matter of moments, she came crashing down into a bush, shifting back to normal with rips in her clothes. The wind of the storm – combined with her lack of muscle memory for flight – had rendered her attempt to catch up to the culprit impossible.

"I'll just need to figure this out a different way," she muttered to herself, her crimson eyes gleaming in utter fury.

Taking a few deep breaths, she willed the red glow to fade into a warm brown colour. She wouldn't be able to blend in with humans here if she failed to conceal her true nature. Humans were understandably fearful of creatures of the night, even if most dismissed the very idea of vampires as a just a myth.

Alana brushed herself off and began walking towards the village. In an hour or so, the rays of sunlight would be peaking over the horizon, and she definitely didn't want to be around to suffer that. Feeling around for a bit, she snatched a black cloak and pulled it up to hide her face. She must have dropped it when in pursuit of the odd bat.

After walking for a while, she arrived at the dirt road of the town, entering in and passing by some comfortable-looking brick buildings stained with the soot of firewood. The patches of grass she passed glistened with the drops of fresh rainfall from the storm that had faded a few minutes before. Alana stuck to the shadows of the buildings, intersecting no humans before coming to a simple house that appeared unwelcoming on the outside.

The yard was overgrown with weeds, and the windows were boarded up. A wooden sign had been placed in full view for anyone to see: *Private Property – do not disturb*. Though humans were always curious, they obeyed this sign, probably getting chills from the feel of the area overall. Good. This was exactly what Alana wanted.

After glancing left, then right, she set off along the pathway to her door, a wooden one with intricate designs of roses and thorns. There might not have been any special meaning to the carvings when they had been made, but Alana enjoyed just the look of things sometimes.

Entering her home, she removed her cloak and hung it on a peg, exhaustion overwhelming her. She collapsed into a comfortable chair, placing her face into her hands and taking several heaving breaths. The gnawing had returned. To ignore the bloodlust would be to black out.

She just couldn't understand it. Why in the world was that man's blood on another bat – and one that was definitely not just some ordinary animal, but a vampire like her?

The only thing she knew was that a vicious vampire was here, and that if she wanted the citizens of this town to remain safe, she would need to help them.

Chapter Two

The next night, Alana found that she was hanging in there, but just barely. She twitched her eye, stumbling to the bathroom and staring at herself in the mirror. Her onyx hair was slightly dishevelled and her eyes were a deep crimson. She stared at her reflection, willing herself to stay in control. This constant battle against the bloodlust was so difficult. She hoped desperately that there had to be a way to control it – a better way than what she was barely managing with.

A loud, snarling rumble from her abdomen indicated that she couldn't ignore this any longer. With a sigh, she dragged herself from the bathroom and into the kitchen, wandering past simple black walls adorned with the occasional picture of decorated temples from a world long ago.

When she arrived at the icebox, she bent down

and opened the unit to pull out two bags of blood.

Making her way to her table, she collapsed shakily, her nostrils flaring and her stomach protesting this *madness*. Ignoring how queasy she felt, she buried her fangs into the plastic. The *pop* of her teeth into the material sounded alike to what it would have been to bite into the skin of a human. But not *quite* the same.

Alana hated the taste and smell. Stale, bitter blood made its way disgustingly down her throat, forcing her to gag a few times. It was long past its best, but had enough nutrients to keep her going. Even though expired blood tasted horrible, at least she would be able to sustain her energy for a few days after consumption. This blood had been thrown away by the medical centre. It was no good for transfusions; either expired or from patients found to be sick after the fact. Alana hoped it was just the former.

Upon finishing the unpleasant task of feeding, she grabbed a parchment and pen, scribbling down her plans for the day.

"Get more bagged blood... hopefully the shortage has been resolved somewhat," she muttered to herself. "Obtain some newspapers, do some research… find the culprit…"

This idea was as solid as it needed to be for now. Besides, she couldn't exactly think straight after having swallowed that disgusting muck. The hunger pangs within her were a stark reminder of her reality. She could devour all the stale blood that she could tolerate but it would never be enough to keep the bloodlust under control.

Things had been even harder for Alana prior to humanity's discovery of transfusion and storing blood. She'd managed for centuries before by leeching off of fresh corpses. It had left her feeling weaker than she was now. At least with the stale blood from the blood bank, despite the unpleasantness, she could remain stronger than she had managed to back then – even if by just a tad.

After several minutes of getting a hold of herself once more, she returned to the bathroom to verify that her gaze was back to normal. Seeing the warm brown of her eyes, she sighed in relief. Grabbing a thick black jacket that she wore over a simplistic grey shirt and dark jeans, Alana headed out into the town once more.

Tonight, the moon was bright with very few

passing clouds. The scent of wet earth hadn't faded quite yet. It blended beautifully with the smell of fresh bread being baked. Alana made her way down the street with her hood pulled up to hide her face. Even if she did bump into someone, it probably wouldn't be a problem due to her retracted fangs.

Speaking of *problems,* however, her nostrils flared as the coppery, delicious scent of blood hit her senses. She narrowed her gaze, her eyes darting to some passing gentlemen who were chatting leisurely. The thudding of their hearts forced shivers to cascade down her spine. She resisted the urge to give a guttural growl, counting to ten several times over in her head to keep herself under control.

The bagged blood had been the bare minimum, and she was feeling that overwhelmingly. Fresh blood, and from the source, was the only way to truly satiate the lust. Alana couldn't *have* that though. The humans were not lesser beings, they were not prey. She refused to tear into an empathetic being. Despite how painful it was, she had mostly been able to stay in control for so many centuries. That cursed *gnawing* was a constant reality check of just how on edge she was on a regular basis.

That shouldn't be the focus right now, she scolded herself, her lips twisting into a scowl as she walked along. She was on a mission, and had to find out about the damage that had been caused by the rogue vampire.

She approached a looming brick building, the well-known library for this town. It confirmed as much with the glittering metallic lettering upon the front entrance. Luckily for Alana, who was a nocturnal creature, this place stayed open late into the night.

Entering the library, she was overwhelmed by the scent of books. Just for a moment, it spared her from the scent of blood rushing through all the humans nearby. She stood there, eyes closed, and took in the smell of old paper and ink. Alana was so lost in it that the clerk's *ahem* caused her to jump somewhat.

"Greetings Alana," she said politely. "Here to mull over the books for a few hours? Not that I mind. You alone might as well be paying for my schooling with how often you visit. I did add some newly published books to the shelf. You know where to look."

Making a mental note to come back and check

out the new material another time, Alana pulled her hood down and provided a bright, relaxed smile to the clerk.

"Oh, thank you. I'm actually researching for a project today," she said with a silken tone.

Centuries alive, Alana had seen other vampires become stone cold. She had never understood that herself; she had always lived in the moment and was open to change, just as long as it was positive. That spark, and that love for life, hadn't burned out yet – and it wasn't about to anytime soon.

Anyway, the clerk helped her to find the latest newspaper. Alana gratefully accepted it and tucked herself into the corner of the library to read. Knowing that business was slow at this time of year, Alana tipped the clerk generously. The clerk had long since stopped insisting that Alana should accept her change.

Having found a nice, quiet spot, Alana began to scan the newspaper, ignoring the gossip and turning straight to the crime reports. She frowned, noting the increase in cases of missing persons. Then, she gulped as her eyes swept over some news that was even more alarming.

The newspaper described animal attacks where pinpricks had been found on corpses. Alana knew better, of course. Vampires were shrouded in superstition, with very few in this town believing in their existence. As the world had progressed and moved on from the past myths, vampires faded into obscurity without complaint. It made hunting far more simplistic. Those who didn't believe weren't equipped for vampire attacks.

Well. I am, Alana thought to herself, furrowing her brow.

She explored the papers for a little while longer before tucking them into her bag and slinging it over her shoulder. With a shaky sigh, she stood up, bidding the clerk a kind farewell before heading out into the night.

She told herself, with a passing thought, that it would be imperative to take care of this issue before someone like the clerk got hurt. She didn't interact with many humans aside from the clerk woman, but people-watching had led her to believe that this was a good little town. Sure, drama sprung up here and there, but innocent people didn't deserve to die by that *fiend's* fangs.

A sinking feeling alerted Alana to the thought that she was just like the culprit. How was she any different, with this lust for blood? Born a monster, that's what she believed, and…

No. I need to focus and stop with the self-hate, for now, at least. People's lives are on the line, she told herself.

As she walked down the road, she licked her lips, her chest heaving as she took in the scent of something delicious.

Hmm… that smells… good… Something I need to find and devour, yes. To feel the silken liquid run down my throat, warm, revitalising…

Blood. Her eyes flashed crimson momentarily, shining in the moonlight. Luckily, there was no one around to catch a glimpse. Someone was bleeding, and their blood was rich with adrenaline. The very few humans walking around at night were blissfully unaware of this. Alana was the only one to catch a whiff of it in the wind since she was a blood drinker.

Darting into the shadows, Alana began to move with supernatural speed, out of view of the humans. She had enough sense to stay safe in that respect, but the closer she got to the scent, the more crazed she became. Soon, she was snarling with beast-like growls as she left the edge of town and charged into the forest.

Just a little longer, then I can feed. No... NO! I can't....

The edges of her vision began to darken, the lust suffocating her. The gnawing in her stomach was in full frenzy, spilling forth like the saliva pouring from her mouth. Her jaw hung open as her delicate fangs sprang out.

The last thing she saw before everything went dark were two figures in a struggle. The last thing she heard was a feminine scream.

Chapter Three

"Let me go! Please! I'm begging you!"

A voice whimpered in Alana's ear. Her fangs were within punctured flesh. A delicious flow of blood was gliding down her throat. When something shook her shoulder, ever so slowly she started to come to her senses. Nostrils flaring, she gasped, her dark hair falling into her face somewhat as she let go of what she was latched onto.

Alana stumbled back, fixing her fading crimson gaze upon a woman with matted brown hair and skin a bit *too* pale. Drawing her tongue over her lips, the vampire's chest heaved as she whimpered and backed away from the wounded woman.

"What have I done?!" Alana cried, her tone one of melancholy.

The woman she'd attacked took several deep

breaths then sat up, pressing her hand to her neck. She wore a simple wool shirt. It had been dyed blue but now had several splotches of crimson upon it. The woman struggled to get to her feet, miraculously standing and leaning against a tree. She appeared to be middle-aged, with a few wrinkles under her eyes.

"...S-so...dizzy..." she whispered before fixing an exhausted gaze upon Alana. "Why did you help me?"

"What?!" Alana asked, shocked.

As she finally surveyed her surroundings, Alana noticed the disturbed dirt in this area. There were deep claw marks in the tree that the human woman was leaning against. The ground and some of the nearby bushes were splattered with blood. The scent of another vampire hung clear in the air but there was no sign of them.

Then, Alana's eyes fell upon a knife. It was *her* knife, glinting silver in the moonlight and stained with the blood of a recent victim. Finally, she turned her gaze back to the woman.

"Why aren't you running in fear from me? I... bit you. Wrongly. I'm sorry," Alana said with sincerity.

"Well, as I said; you helped me. Evidently you don't know *why* yourself. But I was being attacked – ambushed actually – by another monster before you came along. I couldn't see them, just a dark silhouette. I heard guttural growls emitting from the monster, and fangs kept trying to latch onto my flesh. The feeling was like that of trying to fend off a hungry wolf, admittedly," the woman explained.

Alana was becoming increasingly confused.

"How are you so calm about this?" she whimpered, falling to her knees again and burying her face into her hands. "I am so sorry for contributing to that, I don't know what happened, I lost control, I…"

A hand fell upon Alana's shoulder, causing her to flinch. She didn't lift her face from her hands and opted to just listen.

"Hey," the woman muttered. "It's alright. Hold tight... I didn't get to finish my story."

Alana said nothing, baffled and keen to listen. The woman took a deep breath, sinking down into a sitting position.

"Ah. That's better," she said. "I'm still weak on my feet. Where were we? Oh, yes. I was done for. Then… you showed up. Your eyes were a blood red, not that pretty brown that I can see in the moonlight now. Your mouth held fangs, quite like those of my attacker. But you used the claws you have on one hand, and the knife in the other. You then began to mercilessly attack the other monster. When they ran off, you turned on me."

Alana winced, guilt radiating off of her in waves. The woman gently shook the vampire's shoulder.

"You could have ripped my throat out. But you stopped when I begged you. That tells me that you must be different from them."

Mulling this over in her head, Alana slowly nodded, letting out a breath. She placed a hand upon her forehead and sniffled.

"There still must be something more I can do," she said.

"Well, I'm going to assume you're not the cause of the vanishings," the woman said, her voice tinged with deep sadness. "I certainly hope you're not anyway. I've never met… something like you before; it is reassuring to know that while monsters exist, there can be good ones. Are you, perchance, a vampire?"

Knowing the bat was out of the bag, Alana nodded.

"I'm a vampire, yes," she said. "I'm not the cause of the vanishings though – you are correct there as well. I was on my way to start searching for the culprit but I blacked out. Anyway, how did you know?"

"I research folklore, but it appears the myths aren't as imaginary as I thought," the woman replied. "I'm Minerva. My daughter and I were visiting this town, trying to learn more about said folklore. Not many travel these days. But we make a point of doing so – it's our job, after all."

A pit began to form in Alana's stomach. She licked her lips nervously.

"Where is your daughter?" she whispered.

Minerva smiled sadly, bowing her head. Some of her hair fell into her face as she removed her hand from her neck. The bleeding had stopped.

Luckily, Alana hadn't been careless with her bite.

"She's among those who have vanished," Minerva finally said, choking a bit.

The woman had held it together up until this point, but then she burst into tears. She sobbed into her hands and shuddered fiercely. Alana gasped, hesitantly mirroring the woman's prior gesture and placing her hand upon her shoulder.

"We'll find her," she said, firmly.

"Thank you," Minerva replied gratefully.

The woman sighed as she just about managed to compose herself. After a few moments, she stood, wobbling a bit before stabilising herself on a tree. Alana watched carefully, trying not to let the constant feeling of guilt tug at her soul.

"The disappearances seem to be somewhat common right now for this town," said Minerva, suddenly with an authority in her tone. "Eerie happenings are what drew us here in the first place. Never had I thought, as I said, that vampires would be real, but here we are. I'll keep your secret. No one would believe me anyway." Alana felt somewhat relieved to hear this.

The sad smile didn't fade from Minerva's lips, not even when she grew serious.

"Do you think the one who attacked me is the cause of the disappearances?"

Alana narrowed her eyes, deep in thought for a moment.

"Hmm…" she muttered. "Not only did they have the scent of a vampire, but the other day in the woods, I found a corpse."

At the sound of Minerva catching her breath, Alana studied her for a moment before realising that she'd said something particularly unsettling.

"It was a man, probably from another town. It wasn't me who killed them," Alana added awkwardly.

Rather than fixate on any particular fact, Minerva wanted to know more.

"And you think this is relevant?" she asked.

"The man had clearly been attacked by a vampire," said Alana. "He had the classic pinprick bites on his skin and had been drained of most of his blood; I didn't scent it in his veins when I buried him, despite it being everywhere else *but* within him. I wanted to respect the dead and not just leave him there. As I finished covering the grave, I caught the scent of a bat colony. Normally, they eat insects. One of them was covered in *his* blood though. I have a strong suspicion that this is all linked."

The glint of hope in Minerva's eyes had diminished.

"I don't know if my daughter is still alive out there," she said, sighing heavily. "If the vampire got her, then…"

"We can't give up," Alana insisted. "I fought off that vampire, and I'll pursue them until they're gone. Clearly they have no decency or respect for human life – a common trait among my kind."

"What about you?" Minerva questioned with a raised brow. "Why aren't you like that? Are you a young vampire?"

"No. I've been alive for centuries now," Alana replied. "I just don't think like they do. It's a long story."

"Well," Minerva finally said. "If we're going to be working together on this, it looks like I'll have a lot of time to listen."

A light chuckle escaped Alana's lips as she rubbed the back of her neck.

"We should get you some rest first before we head out and start searching again," the vampire said. "Do you have a place to stay? I can offer a bed, if you'd like. Though, considering I'm the reason you're weakened, I wouldn't blame you if you declined."

"I haven't got through life by cowering in fear at inappropriate times," Minerva replied. "As I said, you got to your senses when I begged you to, and here we are talking. You also might be the key to me getting my daughter back. I don't want to lose her."

Minerva's last words came out slightly choked. Alana felt them tug at her heart. The vampire got to her feet, pulling her hood over her head.

"Let's head back," she said. "We can discuss this more at my home."

The journey back to Alana's house was

mercifully uneventful. The moon overhead helped to guide the pair until the soft light of the town aided their sight. Well, Minerva's more than Alana's; Minerva wasn't a creature of the night by any means.

"Dark, simple, sweet. Very respectable, and expected," Minerva muttered on her first impressions of Alana's home.

Not wanting to question what Minerva meant by that, Alana guided her inside and set her up on the couch with a mass of blankets.

"I can stop by the market to pick up food for you. I have none stocked here. You can probably guess why," the vampire said with a light sigh.

"Not a fan of the local cuisine?" Minerva chuckled, but then grew serious and gave a nod. "The blood loss will render me hungry, so that would be much appreciated. Thank you for not just leaving me there. I could tell that you were on edge and afraid of *yourself.* It took a lot of strength, I think, to do what you did."

Shocked, Alana's smile widened brightly.

"It was the right thing to do," she confirmed. "I'll

go and get some food for you immediately. Then, after we've both managed to get some rest, we can start the search for your daughter."

Chapter Four

Alana wandered back into town, the moonlight still glimmering over it. Noticing the starlight that accompanied the menagerie of colours, the vampire found her lips twisting up into a smile. Despite everything that had just happened, she found joy in this setting – and all the more so when the sound of music spilled through the town.

A cascade of violins, drums, and flutes bedazzled the area, alerting Alana to the fact that despite the hour being rather late, humankind nearby wanted to play. As she walked down the road and passed by several people, she could overhear from their conversations that there was a stark contrast between the music and the mood.

"My husband hasn't returned since last night. He wouldn't turn to infidelity, that isn't like him. Where could he be?"

"Has anyone see the baker, you know, the one with the famous cookies? They apparently haven't opened shop for three days now."

"My neighbour's son was chopping wood one night recently, but never came back. He could be drunk in a back alley, but something tells me there are darker forces involved."

"I don't believe in monsters, but if I did, that would explain both the weird animal attacks, and the vanishings. This ain't the work of a wolf, that's for damn sure."

Placing a hand on her forehead, Alana winced, travelling towards the music primarily now to drown out such conversation. Her advanced hearing made it easy to pick up the worries of the townsfolk. It didn't help her anxiety one bit. Although the festivities in celebration of the autumn equinox were in full bloom, the wind was noticeably colder for the time of year. There was something about it that just didn't feel right.

The sky darkened for a moment, causing the vampire's gaze to turn upwards. She spotted a swirl of movement, then clocked the colony of bats above, snatching up mosquitoes and moths. The occasional crow let out a harsh *caw* of disapproval, but otherwise, they were left undisturbed.

Alana couldn't help but study the winged creatures for a moment, trying to spot the odd one out again. Despite being put off by the colony as it circled in abundance above her, she could not detect blood other than that which rushed through the veins of the townsfolk.

As a matter of fact, the gnawing was silent for now. A sinking feeling told Alana that this was due to her having attacked Minerva. It had sated the need to hunt; she'd taken enough blood to satisfy the hunger. Selfishly, Alana almost felt *glad* about this. Here she was, wandering through the town, for the first time in a while able to focus on things like the music rather than the sound of heartbeats.

She was determined to buy Minerva the very best of savoury dishes here, tasty and nourishing. Thank goodness that festivity brought food, for the vampire easily found exactly what she was looking for.

****

The scent of bread and warm chicken stew

billowed throughout Alana's house, fresh and mouthwatering. There was an abundance of drinking water too, something that would help to rehydrate Minerva after the loss of blood. She was sitting up on the couch, reading the newspapers that Alana had provided for more context.

"The town is getting riled up. We need to be careful, considering what you are. They could start believing the myths as truth soon," Minerva said.

As Alana entered the room, Minerva smiled, flaring her nostrils at the inviting smell of good food.

"That smells delicious. Did you get that from the night market? Those places always have good food," Minerva sighed nostalgically. "Maybe being bitten by a vampire and having my senses heightened in an instant has been worth it after all."

Alana furrowed her brow and placed the food on the table for Minerva, taking a seat in an old chair across from her. They were surrounded by dark colours of the cold variety, like blues and purples. Still, Alana reached over and lit a candle on the table, recalling that Minerva couldn't see in the dark quite as well.

Alana sat back in her chair, studying Minerva.

"I'm still taken aback by how calm you are about all of this," Alana admitted.

Minerva chuckled. She reached over and plucked the stew from the table, resting it on her lap. Stirring it with a silver spoon for a moment, she took a sip and hummed.

"Ah, this soup is delectable. Thank you," she said. "I'm calm because I'm someone who keeps moving forwards. Why live in fear of new information? I'm merely grateful that now I *know* and can be more prepared for it. Speaking of new information, what's your name by the way?"

"Alana," the vampire replied, relaxing further in Minerva's presence.

"What a beautiful name," Minerva commented.

The two of them sipped at their stew contentedly for a moment.

"I want to ask you about something that's on my mind," Minerva said. "You say you've been alive for many centuries. How can it be that you're not bored with life? How have you not lost that spark?"

In silence, Alana considered the question. She hadn't given it much thought before. She rarely interacted with other vampires. When she had, she'd noticed that, over the years, most of them had become as emotionless as stone. Many questioned the point of their long existence. How had she managed to avoid that? The more she thought about it now, the more the answer seemed simple.

"I live in the moment," the vampire confessed. "My life is full of books and searching. The world is always changing, so why should I remain stagnant? The old me still exists, but it evolves. I think those who lose themselves over the centuries aren't creatures of change. Being alive for so long, some just get stuck in the past. But that's not exciting, and that's no way to live. For example, all of the time, there are people out there who are writing something new; not one story will ever be the same. This also applies to music. They are both things that I love."

"And what do you say to those who tell you that every story has *already* been told, and that every melody is just a variation of those from before?" Minerva asked, fascination in her tone. "You have knowledge of so much, after all. Surely you encounter a lot of repetition?"

"While some truth rings in that, it is only partially so. Look at how our world advances around us in every way. I don't believe I will *ever* know all there is to know about music, culture, science. As humanity continues to evolve, I'll be right there alongside it, adding to my knowledge as well. I don't retain everything. In fact, much of it is relatively forgettable. That doesn't matter though. I remember enough. And, most of all – like I said, I live in the moment and I look to the future; I'm not stuck in the past."

Minerva gave a nod, beaming at the vampire.

"I like how you think, Alana. It is very wise. You have a good soul. Many think that vampires are damned for all eternity. I would argue against that; here you are, proving that concept wrong."

Gasping, Alana reached up to wipe away a tear, furrowing her brow and giving a soft smile.

"Hearing that means the world to me. Thank you. I just wish I could get rid of this horrible bloodlust. It's why I went berserk and bit you. My kind… we have the need to hunt; to consume the blood of *your kind.* We are the cause of so much misery."

"So is humanity," Minerva replied plainly, giving a dark scowl. "If there's anything I picked up during my travels, it's that no one is perfect. You're far more respectful than many of the fellow humans I've dealt with. That's saying something, considering you bit me."

Alana looked away, her cheeks tinged with embarrassment.

"Do not worry yourself on that matter," Minerva said. "We have already established that you are strong enough to stop. Speaking of which, the other one you chased off. Did you do anything special, or did you just use those claws of yours? I would never have expected that a simple knife could chase off another vampire."

"Silver is deadly to our kind," Alana explained.

The vampire withdrew the knife from her side. It was still stained with blood. Minerva didn't wince. Instead, she studied it from a distance for a moment before nodding.

"I use this only in dire circumstances, for self defence, or what you saw there," Alana added, carefully putting the knife back in its sheath.

"I understand. Perhaps I should get one of those for myself," Minerva chuckled.

Alana smiled, appreciating Minerva's sense of humour. The woman couldn't forget her worries though. Sighing, she looked towards the wall, entirely lost in thought.

"Calm as I am, I still feel so much despair. I just hope we can find my daughter. I hope she's safe. If not… I hope we can give her the peace that she deserves."

"We'll find her," Alana promised firmly.

The vampire's warm brown eyes were almost blazing. They didn't glow red though, for she was not hungry or angry.

"I pray that you are right," Minerva said, her sad gaze meeting Alana's determined one. "But I also will keep my expectations realistic. Regardless,

I know we will do all that we can within our power."

Minerva brushed her hand through her hair and closed her eyes. She settled in, pulling the blankets over herself.

"You have a good night, Alana. Once again, thank you for your help with this matter. Hopefully we will cover much ground tomorrow."

The vampire stood up, clearing the table and giving a nod.

"Definitely. Rest well, Minerva."

With that, Alana retired for the night, her thoughts wild and swimming this way and that. The human she'd attacked was far more understanding than she felt she deserved. She *had* to find Minerva's daughter alive. It was the least she could do for the woman after having lost control.

Her thoughts shifted to the vampire that had initially attacked Minerva. Alana couldn't recall having fended them off. The only thing that she could remember with clarity was the moment the woman had begged her to stop drinking. When she had arrived on the scene, she hadn't been able to discern *any* features, just a shadow. The bloodlust had clouded all reasoning from there, something she cursed, for if only she had been able to decipher *something*.

Putting that thought aside for now, Alana drifted off into a troubled sleep.

Chapter Five

At the next sunset, the two were off, Minerva a little more steady than before. "Thank you for the spare knife," she said to Alana. "It's quite a shame that wooden stakes aren't as effective."

"A stake to the chest would be agonisingly crass," Alana admitted, shuddering. "But yes, a silver knife is much better for defence."

They journeyed through the woods for a while. Their aim was to be as quiet as possible, just to play it safe.

Like a wave did the scent of fresh blood hit Alana, but she found herself resisting the urge to go berserk. Although the gnawing hunger in her stomach continued to remind her of its presence, her attack on Minerva had sated it just enough for her to be able to keep her urges under control. For now.

"I detect something," Alana muttered.

Her words caused Minerva to tense up.

"Wow! You're like a bloodhound," the woman joked, trying to calm her nerves.

Passing some pine trees as the sun dipped further under the horizon, Alana gave a low growl as the scent grew stronger. Soon, they came upon a clearing, much to their deep dismay.

From metal pikes coming out of the ground, there were skeletons that had been picked clean of all flesh. They were held together by metal pins, no doubt. Some were missing several bones here and there. All had a skull and a rib cage. Shocked, Alana fell to her knees, struggling to take it all in.

"The Beast of Temes," Minerva whispered.

Too shocked to do anything else, she got down on her knees next to Alana. Neither of them had ever seen anything like it.

"Alana, are you alright?"

Alana's eyes were glowing deep red, no doubt

due to the grisly scene and the strong scent of blood all around. In fact, the metal itself was tinged with it.

"What do you mean?" the vampire finally asked.

"This is the reason my daughter and I came here in the first place. There were rumours of a serial killer who had recently engaged in *this* behaviour, who was thought to have vanished a century ago. We were doing some research on the story. It had been built up to be an urban legend. Clearly though, this is reality," Minerva replied.

She made her way to a nearby pine tree. Slumping against it, she covered her face with her hands. Softly, she began to cry, shuddering from how heavily this all weighed on her heart.

"This is so much to handle. What if… what if my daughter…"

Alana quickly darted over, hesitantly placing a hand on Minerva's shoulder. The woman didn't pull away from the vampire. Instead, she stayed there for a moment, trying to compose herself.

Distracted, Alana widened her eyes as the scent

of another vampire hit her. She stood up and let out a surprised snarl, causing Minerva to tense.

"There is danger here," Alana scowled. "I can sense it. Keep your knife at the ready. Do you mind if I follow the scent? There is only one right now. I can run them down before they get to *us* first."

"Be careful," Minerva pleaded in a muffled voice, her face still buried in her hands.

With that assurance, Alana was off, darting through the woods towards the scent of another vampire. She hadn't seen a vampire around here for many years, never mind a highly aggressive one. Would she be able to match them in combat properly, especially in her partially-starved state? Pushing her concerns to the back of her mind, she pressed onwards, proceeding closer and closer to the other vampire.

Darting between the pikes that held the skeletons, Alana's shoulder accidentally slammed into one. She had to leap to the side to avoid a loose humerus that came crashing down. In the distance she could now see the silhouette of someone. The overwhelming scent of blood told her that this was her target. She braced herself.

Launching at the other vampire, she sank her fangs into their flesh.

A masculine yell rose into the air as claws sank lightly into Alana's cheek.

Slash! She felt blood start to drip from her neck. It was dangerously close to being a much deeper wound due to the other vampire's claws.

Slash! She hit back. Claw marks formed on the cheeks of the enemy vampire.

Slash! Blood splattered everywhere as claws ripped across her shirt and into her chest.

Within an instant, Alana was down on the ground, under the weight of the enemy vampire. Clawed hands held her down by the shoulders, and fangs were bared in her face. Wisps of his raven-coloured hair fell into her face as he let out a long hiss. The tanned skin of his face was stained with his own and Alana's blood. Amongst all of this though, there wasn't even a trace of a scent of *human* blood on him.

"It seems I've discovered the Temes Beast," he bellowed in a deep voice. "Any last words before I rip your throat out, you disgrace?"

Alana growled loudly, thrashing and snapping her fangs. The male vampire pinning her to the ground suddenly let out an agonised roar and rolled off. The handle of a silver knife stuck out from under his shoulder blade. Standing there, silhouetted against the moon, was Minerva, her hand shaking. The woman's eyes fell upon her own hand, as if entirely surprised that she'd stabbed the vampire attacking Alana.

"Me? The Beast?" Alana spluttered out, finally finding her voice. "I'm nothing of the sort. You are the cause of this! Aren't you? Other vampires do not belong here!"

The male vampire reached out behind him and pulled the knife from his back, clenching his fist. Then, he tossed it to Minerva's feet, his red eyes glowing brightly in sheer fury. Minerva took a step back, her eyes widening and her heart pounding.

"You came from the shadows and attacked me while I was investigating. Though, this human is an entirely new development. Do tell me. If you are not the beast, then what are you doing here?" he asked, his voice dripping with distrust.

His eyes darted from Minerva to Alana as he

crossed his arms, his entire body rigid.

"*You* were investigating? That's what we're here for as well. I had no idea there were others on the search like me," Alana said, her voice tinged with suspicion.

Offended, the male vampire rolled his shoulders back and scoffed, wincing from the knife wound.

"Yes. Might I remind you that *you* attacked *me* first?" he growled. "There is a disgrace wandering around here, tormenting the humans. They have already lashed out at me from the shadows. I couldn't properly formulate a counterattack and they fled into the night. They have an uncalled-for aggression and obsession, as you can see here."

He gestured around, his red eyes flashing in disgust before falling on Alana again.

"You say you are nothing of the sort," he continued. "And I am inclined to believe you, considering your friend stabbed me in the back on your behalf."

Minerva moved to stand behind Alana, just to be safe.

"Sir, can I have my knife back?" the human asked.

The male vampire blinked once, twice, and then sighed. He crouched down and snatched up the knife, then calmly approached the two.

"Here. My name is Michael."

Hesitantly, Minerva reached out and accepted the knife. She quickly went back to stand behind Alana upon receiving it.

"I'm Alana," the female vampire replied, allowing her body to relax just slightly. "It looks like we're on the same side. But what brings you here? And do you know what happened with all of *this?*"

Michael straightened up, reaching behind him to rub unsuccessfully at the wound on his back. It was *just* out of reach. Having to accept this, he let out a sigh and fixed his eyes upon Alana. He reached up to stroke the stubble on his chin as he spoke.

"I investigate nefarious members of our kind and put a stop to their activity. They threaten our existence by making humans more aware of us.

That alone would not be a problem, but of course, a case of mass violence always is. I want to live harmoniously with humankind," he explained. "Things like *this* only contribute to fear, hatred, and an increase in vampire hunters. In the long run, none of that is healthy for our society."

"Why haven't I heard of this?" Alana asked, her eyes wide with shock. "And what of my bloodlust?"

"Clearly you have a lot to be informed about," Michael sighed. "But we will put that aside for now. We need to find this beast. The entire town of Temes is at stake."

He looked around the landscape, making a note of the skeletons clicking eerily in the wind.

58

Chapter Six

The three walked further into the woods. As they did so, they came across even more pikes adorned with skeletons.

"Why is it set up like this? Like a showcase?" Alana whispered. "Who would do such a thing?"

"There are those among us with sadistic minds. This is not exclusive to just vampires," Michael muttered, shaking his head. "In fact, many vampires learn from humans; who else could hurt a human better than humanity itself?"

Minerva, walking on the other side of Alana, turned her head to peer at Michael, and gave a light nod.

"You speak the truth," she said. "My daughter and I were scrutinised for our research and work. Sometimes we were even threatened. We never stayed in one place for long enough to be accused of witchcraft. People these days throw that accusation around so thoughtlessly and condemn others to death in doing so. Mankind has some awful qualities, but some very good ones too; a melting pot of chaos."

Michael looked around, and then pointed to Alana with a soft smile. At least the trio now felt a little more comfortable with each other.

"This also applies directly to vampirekind," he said. "Look around us, and then look at your friend there. I do not know how you came to be working together, but it warms my heart to know that there are more with my mindset walking the earth."

Alana mulled this over in her mind, deciding that she was glad to have met Michael – despite the scuffle they'd had. Her wounds were already healing, as were his. Having been stabbed with silver would slow the male vampire's healing process but luckily, the knife hadn't been driven into him too deeply.

"Perhaps we should regroup and discuss our plans. Refusal won't offend, but you're welcome to stay at my home," Alana explained. "We could dress your shoulder wound there."

"Your house is rather large," Minerva said, sounding amused. "Why am I not surprised that you have room for one more?"

Alana's face flushed in embarrassment. Her eyes darted upwards to gaze at the starlit sky.

"Whilst I don't embrace all aspects of my vampiric heritage," she said. "I can't deny my accumulation of wealth."

A chuckle was shared between the three, and soon enough they were walking through the woods, back towards Alana's home. Alana stole a glance towards Michael, who had lapsed into silence as they wandered. A squirrel paused in their path, staring at them with an alert expression before moving on. Michael focussed upon the animal for a moment, watching it scurry about and into the shadows.

"What makes you different like me?" Alana suddenly asked.

Startled, the male vampire turned his head to look at Alana.

"What is the point of living forever if you allow yourself to become nothing; a hollow shell of your previously vibrant and beautiful self? I have been alive for a few centuries. The adoration I have for the creatures around us has never died, and it never will."

Minerva looked between Michael and Alana. It delighted her to hear both vampires echo that part of themselves to each other.

"I feel Alana still has some accepting to do," the human said in a careful tone. "Do you hate what you are, Michael?"

"I do not," the male vampire said, letting out a soft breath. "Wallowing in self-hatred got me nowhere. I make do with what I can. Alana here will find herself, however. I am sure of it."

"I *am* right here, you know," Alana grumbled.

As they entered the town, it became clear that the festivities from the previous night had died down. The atmosphere was rather peaceful. Alana led the group to her home. Upon entry, she showed Michael to a simple room with a large bed and several fluffy blankets.

"I have a room for you as well," she said to Minerva. "You don't have to stay on the couch."

Minerva declined, saying that the couch was just fine.

"You won't need to feed anytime soon, will you?" Alana asked, looking at Michael.

"I am sated, for now," said the male vampire, shaking his head. "I have my own ways of feeding my bloodlust."

Alana shot him a questioning stare.

"I will explain more tomorrow," he said. "Right now though, I need to rest."

He reached over his shoulder and rubbed towards the wound again, causing Alana to gasp.

"Oh, I apologise! You're right, we need rest. Indeed, we'll talk more in the morning. Rest well, sir," she said.

Turning away and walking to her own room, Alana bid Minerva goodnight. She closed her bedroom door and collapsed upon a bed with lavender blankets, her chest heaving and her mind swirling from the day.

The images of the skeletons on the pikes

bombarded her thoughts, as did the sound of clattering bones blowing in the frigid wind. A reminder of far more than death. She shuddered. Some humans were granted a peaceful death in their sleep. Some lived rather long, and old age eventually closed its jaws upon them. But that wasn't the case for those displayed as skeletons.

When Alana closed her eyes, she could only see her own kind ripping the throats out of humans, laughing as a river of blood flowed freely throughout the streets. Shadows with deep red eyes, gorging themselves on the inevitably delicious. How could she bear to be the same as them?

Her thoughts turned to the wars that humanity had so often engaged in, and of all the horrible things they had done. *Does that make every single human irredeemable and evil? Of course not. There is so much good in mankind as well.*

As she fell asleep, her thoughts faded to Michael and the way that he had looked at that squirrel as they had been walking home. He had stared at the creature with a mixture of curiosity and adoration, like a little boy looking at an interesting bug. It was a feeling that Alana could relate to – like that which she experienced when enjoying a good book.

Finally, Alana thought about Minerva. The woman was convinced that some vampires could be good. Alana considered how it would be good to embrace Minerva's optimism in that regard. Despite the woman not having been alive for even half as long as most vampires, her wisdom was inspiring.

Giving a yawn and stretching out her arms, Alana settled down for a good sleep.

So many unanswered questions. How much do I know about myself, really?

****

The next morning, Alana awoke with a horrible gnawing feeling in her gut. She groaned and rolled out of bed with a *thump,* heading over to the kitchen to check in the icebox. With a sinking feeling, she realised that she hadn't checked to see if the medical centre had any expired blood for her to snag.

A loud grumble from her stomach indicated that she was right to be worried. Someone cleared their throat behind her, causing her to hiss and whirl. It was Michael. He studied her reaction for a moment, raising his brow before speaking. He didn't bother hiding his fangs in front of Alana, though he knew to do so when wandering the town.

"Good morning. I assume you seek blood?" he asked, his tone relatively relaxed.

Pausing, Alana gave a curious nod, especially when he reached over his shoulder and brought forwards his bag. He approached the table in the centre of the room, spilling the contents out and causing Alana to gasp.

"Blood bags! You use them too?" Alana asked, rhetorically of course.

With a shrug, Michael snatched up one of them, leaving plenty for the female vampire. He promptly dug in, sinking his fangs into the plastic and drinking quickly. Not even a drop was lost – he was far less messy than Alana. Taking his offer to heart, she grabbed one bag, then two, for herself.

She noticed straight away that the blood wasn't at room temperature and that it wasn't stale. Instead, it was *warm* and it tasted rich. In harmony with her hunger, the silken substance flowed smoothly down her throat, revitalising her to the very core. A cat-like purr came from the pit of her chest as she fed. She couldn't help but close her eyes during this process. It was *almost* perfect. Almost.

Relieved and satisfied, she set the empty bags aside, letting out a sigh. Unlike Michael, she'd made a mess of things, as she always did.

"What was that?" she asked.

After a pause, she started to panic. *That was fresh blood. How did he…*

"Willing donors," Michael said, cutting off her concerned thought process.

His tone was almost one of boredom, as if Alana should know this. There was just the tiniest hint of amusement in there too though.

"As I said," he continued. "There is clearly much that you need to learn, Alana. I am also well aware that no matter how much fresh blood is devoured, the hunting instinct will always be there. It can be satiated by willing donors though. I know of a few in this town, but they keep themselves anonymous. I don't know how long you've been here, but if it's been a while, it surprises me that you've never found them."

"I don't get out much," she admitted.

"I see. Hiding from yourself for many years, I assume?" Michael asked, putting the rest of the bags away. "Well, hopefully – once the issue in this town has been taken care of – you will be made well aware of how our kind can make things work these days."

At that moment, Minerva entered the kitchen, gasping and placing her hand over her heart for a moment.

"Alana! Michael! Warn a woman before you make a mess! Well, Alana, anyway; I think most of that is yours," the human woman grumbled.

Alana's cheeks were red with embarrassment.

"There's no time to lose," Minerva said, motioning to the vampires. "We have much work to do. We need to get moving and start looking for that beast."

Alana and Michael exchanged a look, nodded to one another, then looked back to Minerva.

"Yes," said Alana. "We're ready. Let's go and find your daughter."

Chapter Seven

The trio made their way through the town as the sun dipped under the horizon once again.

"I might as well be a vampire now," Minerva muttered to herself. "What with how active I am at night."

Alana had to stifle a chuckle at that, sympathising with the poor woman.

Into the woods they went again, the pine trees looming almost threateningly. Though many squirrels scurried past, Michael paid them no attention. There were bigger things at stake and distractions would not do.

As they passed by the pikes with skeletons, Alana gasped, noticing that there were more than before. Two more had been added, swaying in the wind and creaking their dark, dead "music".

Alana stared up into the eye sockets of one of the impaled skulls. She wondered what torment they must have gone through right before their death. She made a mental note to suggest taking every last skeleton down once the beast had been dealt with. Finding them was top priority now. Still though, the dead needed to be respected, and displaying them like this was sick.

With no evidence of the beast nearby, the group grew silent. As the search continued, there appeared to be something flickering in the distance. Alana narrowed her gaze and drew in a breath, exhaling sharply.

"The scent of smoke," she said. "It must be coming from torchlight. Out here though? Why?"

At this point, the group had wandered deeper into the woods and away from the impaled skeletons. Minerva stared off into the distance as a cold wind billowed through the air, causing her to shiver slightly. Something told Alana that the woman wasn't just cold though.

"You know when I mentioned that the townsfolk were starting to get more on edge?" the human woman said. "There had been talk of a search. I didn't think much of it at the time, but after having seen so many skeletons now, I'm certain that this is beyond the point of crisis."

"This is not good," Michael muttered. "From my past experiences, a fearful group of humans is an angry one. We need to be on our guard."

Alana, Michael and Minerva endeavoured to walk away from the torches. The light kept drawing closer though. In addition, the barking of hounds could be heard paired with various bits of shouting.

"They're going to catch up with us soon if we don't start moving faster," Alana said with an edged tone. "Maybe we can divert them away from our trail."

"Maybe we could explain the situation to them?" Minerva suggested.

The two vampires frowned and shook their heads.

"It was worth a shot to suggest," said the human. "Let's go."

Ever closer did the torches from the distance

glide, and ever louder did the hounds bark. The wind billowed stronger than before, blowing Alana's hair forwards and carrying the scent of the humans closer to her. Things had been difficult enough with just Minerva next to her. Now though, the clawing within her stomach had grown even stronger.

Alana let out an alarmed growl. Michael's eyes fell upon her, and she winced, not comfortable with being under scrutiny.

"When did you last hunt your blood meal?" he asked, concerned. "The bags do not satiate that, it will claw and bite until it emerges and…"

"THE HOUNDS SCENT THEM! WE CAN FINALLY PUT AN END TO THIS!" a townsman called out, much to the shock and dismay of the trio.

Alana quickened her pace, turning her head to look over her shoulder before feeling an arm shoot out to stop her. Michael had put a halt to both her and Minerva, and with good reason.

When Alana turned to look ahead, she realised that she'd almost slammed right into a large wall of rock. In fact, as she turned her head up towards the moon, she gasped, noticing the edge of a cliff. The towering landmark before them would be impossible to climb.

Alana looked left, then right, observing other landmarks. There was a valley on one side, and another mountain of rock on the other. The three of them were trapped. She turned, hearing her heart pound as the mob drew closer.

The torchlight illuminated the features of several angry humans, sparking Alana to recall the times she had encountered this exact scenario in many of the books that she'd read. She had never expected to be on the receiving end of an angry mob, but here they were.

Minerva stepped forwards, motioning for the two vampires to stand behind her.

"Hello there," she said, addressing the crowd nervously. "We are out investigating this matter as well. There really is no need to storm in here and corner us like this. It's rather frightening."

The gentleman leading the mob narrowed his eyes and stepped forwards, addressing Minerva.

"We've reports of monsters in these woods,

prowling the night to devour flesh. So many have gone missing, and we are done with sitting around and just letting it happen. If you folk are innocent, then why would you have a problem with us?"

He withdrew a vial. Alana recognised it immediately. She had faced off against many vampire hunters in her time. She knew full well that inside it, there was holy water. There were flecks of silver within the water itself, apparently part of an old ritual of sorts that ended up working against vampires in the end. The silver alone wouldn't do much unless it punctured flesh, but the "blessed" part of the ritual – however that happened – caused the silver to become toxic upon touch.

Splash!

The skin on Alana's arm sizzled as the water splashed against it, the chemical substance already burning strongly. She shrieked in agony, the burning sensation similar to what she assumed felt like a severe allergic reaction. Michael hissed as a vial was uncorked and splashed against him as well. He managed to shield his face, but like Alana, was hit on the arm.

The only one of the three who wasn't affected was, unsurprisingly, Minerva. She gasped and removed a handkerchief from her bag and began to vigorously rub away at the substance on Alana's arm.

"As we suspected," the gentleman who'd used the cruel tactic snarled out. "They are burned by the concoction! The monsters are *right here before us!*"

The townsfolk started to close in on the trio.

"How do you know this is not a simple allergy?! What is that chemical mix that you've got there?!" Minerva snapped, whirling to face the townsfolk. "Please do not tell me that you deny science! I know Temes is accepting of change, and moving forwards! Surely you know of allergens! Your victims might be allergic, but I am not! What proof do you have that this reveals they are monsters?!"

The gentleman sneered and brought the torch closer to Minerva.

"Because of their eyes," he said. "Look at their eyes!"

Both Alana and Michael's eyes, when illuminated by the flame, flickered like those of a predator. Indeed, the gleam was beyond anything that could belong to a human. Not only that, but in her panic, Alana's eyes were now a blood red. The heartbeats of all the people around her were clouding her thoughts, pounding in her head, tempting her to frenzy and gorge upon *everyone's* blood.

No… this would confirm their beliefs. I will not give in, and I will not bow to this need to hunt.

She clenched her stomach, letting out a low snarl.

"Minerva," she shouted. "It might be best for you to stand down. I would not want you hurt on our behalf."

"No," Minerva said firmly, turning to look back to the townsfolk. "Listen here. While one did attack me, she aided me in recovery afterwards. The attack was *accidental.* She is innocent and only wants to help. This gentleman was *also* looking for the beast when we stumbled upon him. Fight fire with fire. How exactly do you know that these two are monsters? And anyway, I thought Temes dismissed the idea of monsters merely as folklore?"

The head of the mob put a hand behind his head, deep in thought. He stared Minerva down, recognising that her eyes were not gleaming. She was a human too, and in this situation, definitely needed to be heard. Though she could be conspiring against them, her words could ring true.

"We did," he admitted. "Until the vanishings started to increase. The youngest of us snatched from their place of safety. Workers in the night on maintenance tasks, gone without a trace. A newcomer approached those of us searching for answers. We were shown reality by her collection of fangs. She told us of vampires, and how to defeat them. She said that for a long time, she had been working to put a stop to the madness. Then… she showed us the pikes. Decorated like trees on a holiday, as if they were meant to have bedazzling lights, but really, draped with skeletons. We didn't even know if the holy water would work. And clearly, it has. We see it in their eyes."

His stare fixed upon Alana, and he cleared his throat, his voice raising.

"No more lies," he continued to insist. "Show us your teeth, vampire. We see the truth in your eyes, and we will see it in your fangs."

"How will this buy my innocence?" Alana asked sceptically, exchanging a glance with Michael.

"Honesty buys much, girl," the man muttered.

Alana had no choice. She peeled her lips upwards to flash her fangs. There was a murmur among the townspeople. Their worst fears had been confirmed.

"You know the vampires of legend. You know their strength," Minerva said. "The two here could have dismantled me, and they could well rip many of *you* to shreds as well. Your fears are confirmed, but what now? Here I am in one piece. I have no reason to lie to any of you here. Why would I defend a monster that seeks to harm my own kind?"

More murmurs rippled through the crowd, sparking a hot debate amongst smaller groups within it. Many fragments of conversation were caught by Alana as they spoke.

"That woman could be working with the monsters."

"But why? For what purpose? What is there to gain by working with vampires?"

"Witchcraft, maybe?"

Catching much of this, Minerva shouted in frustration. Alana and Michael exchanged a startled glance. Shocked into silence, the crowd's attention turned to the distraught woman, who had strands of hair falling into her face as she bowed her head in thought.

The uncomfortable silence ended when Minerva gave a choked sob.

"I've worked so hard to hold it together," she said. "I need to remain strong. But you folk need to realise. This is not an instance of witchcraft. I am of sound mind. I just want to find my daughter. She is missing. I love her with all of my heart. She and I came here together in search of knowledge. If that means working with those who you folk consider to be monsters, then so be it. Even in the short time I've known Alana, I've been made aware that she is *not* a monster. She has a *heart*. Michael has been out here searching as well, taking time out to look for the killer you all have come to despise. You don't have to believe me. But… I just want my daughter back.

I just want her back from the real monster."

Burying her face in her hands, Minerva began to cry. Now, the tension in the air could almost be cut with a knife.

Despite everything that was happening, Alana was distracted by something else. The familiar clawing within her stomach had intensified and nothing could silence it. And then it dawned on her; she realised that she was scenting something familiar. *Minerva... is she bleeding? No... but I can smell blood that's so similar to hers... Wait a moment...*

Without warning, Alana gasped and placed a hand on Minerva's shoulder.

"Her scent! I have your daughter's scent! I need to find her!" she said. "Stay here, Michael. Tell everyone here what you told us when we first met; about members of our kind who do *not* support the mindless slaughter. There's no time to lose. I can scent her! She is near!"

Alana didn't care whether anyone would follow her or not. She was locked onto the scent of Minerva's bloodline; blood so similar, yet just slightly different.

The daughter was bleeding, and Alana had to find her before it was too late.

Chapter Eight

Crashing through the woods, her ears ringing and her senses screaming at her to feed, Alana snarled out, cursing that *gnawing* feeling. This was the worst time for it to be chanting within her train of thought. The cold, billowing wind intensified, blowing her hair back as she ran. The scent of her target grew ever-stronger.

Bursting into the clearing adorned with several pikes, Alana noticed the new display immediately. This pike displayed just a single, punctured skull. The final bits of flesh upon it were swarming with flies. It was just as rancid as the other impaled skeletons nearby. The vampire's stomach clenched as she realised something about this display that she hadn't before; they were *territory markers*.

Determined to find the source of the scent, she did not have to search for very long at all. Before her, she could see another vampire crouched over a human. As Alana approached, she could make out the vampire's features. The blonde hair cascading down her back was splotched with the deep crimson of her victims. A wavy blue dress, also stained with blood, bloomed out in the wind. Her ivory skin was covered in laceration scars, many of which dotted her arms. Within her grasp was a young woman, perhaps in her early twenties – the age that Alana appeared to be.

The feeding vampire presented as being a couple of decades older. There was an ethereal beauty to her that could be seen when she pulled away from her victim to fix her pitch-black gaze upon Alana. Clarity struck Alana right then, forcing the darkness around her vision to disperse.

Is that how my eyes look when I lose control?

The feeding vampire smirked, flashing her feline-like fangs at Alana. Then, her smooth melodic voice rang out, caressing Alana's mind with danger.

"Hello there, friend. I remember you. I had fun fighting you the last time. But... care to join me now?"

Shocked, Alana took a step back, her eyes widening in fury.

Did she just call me "friend"? What does she mean, "last time"?

"We aren't friends," Alana commanded, her eyes blazing a deep red. "Let that woman go. *Now.*"

A chiming laughter rang out from the enemy vampire. She then tilted her head.

"Aww, are you some kind of hero? You're here sticking up for our *prey?* Are you not even a real vampire, hmm? We are the monsters of legend. Perhaps you should start acting like it. By refusing to accept my offer to share, it makes you worthless," the vampire purred.

Without warning did she seem to appear before Alana – no doubt having used her speed to get up close. She put her face right up to Alana's.

"My dear, have you ever met Temes' beast?" the dishevelled blonde spoke in a warped tone. "Do you see my beautiful collection? Such pretty little trinkets. A homage to the beauty of death. The recognition that they are mortal... and that we are not."

Slash! Blood spattered out from Alana's cheek as claws ripped through her flesh. The wounds dealt here were immediately far deeper than those from her scuffle with Michael. This time though, Alana was ready, and she was angry.

Alana's hand lunged downwards for her knife and, as quickly as a striking snake, she stabbed it into the beast's side. A flow of blood poured out, causing the enemy vampire to snarl out in sheer anger. Despite that, her melodic, gorgeous voice continued to taunt and jab.

"We are the same. Can't you see?! Look around you! Look at my work! The gorgeous reality of the world, all for everyone to see! Now is the age of the vampire! And you will either accept that, or be left behind."

The beast lunged for Alana again, claws glinting in the moonlight.

The two vampires clashed hard, fangs clamping onto one another's shoulders, ripping out chunks of flesh.

Alana's knife was an instrument of death and an extension of herself. Many stab wounds littered the beast, causing her to grunt and roar primitively. There was no hesitation, yet this task was far from simple, and it was far from a clear victory. Though Alana had silver, the ravenous beast's cruelty and hunger edged her forwards, like a puppet on many strings of sin.

And still, the beast kept speaking.

"It was I who sent those townsfolk after you. They are so easy to manipulate and fool! A feeble ally in their state of panic, but useful nonetheless against you and yours. You leech! To know that some of *my kind* do not share my views; it won't do. *It won't do!*"

The beast was starting to make progress, pushing Alana towards a tree and shoving her up against it. Her fangs still dripped with the blood of Minerva's daughter as she smirked darkly.

"You won't get anywhere in this world if you aren't cruel, my dear," she taunted. "Look around this place, darling! The *cruelty* of nature is on full display! Why should we be any different? Why should the spider pity the moth? That is life. That is death. That is *vampire.* What a pity that I don't have the tolerance to teach you."

A deep voice rang out from behind the beast, and

blazing red eyes met Alana's. Suddenly, the beast was thrown off and away from Alana, and Michael stood there with his still-healing flesh from the chemical burns. Flashes of torchlight flickered behind him, as did the angered shouts of the townspeople.

"Alana! You've wounded her greatly," Michael exclaimed.

The beast composed herself and bunched up her muscles, ready to pounce.

"I'll check on the wounded woman. You finish the beast off," Michael quickly commanded to Alana. "You're powerful enough to do this, and you have backup as a last resort."

Before Michael could get to the wounded human woman, the beast let out a gurgled snarl and lunged for him. Tackling him down from behind, she latched onto the back of his throat and began to tear into his back. She refused to let go even as Alana began to resume her attacks.

The shouting swirled all around Alana. The frantic beating of hearts caused her to cry out in hunger. The gnawing in her stomach continued to increase as the scent of fear and blood tainted the air. She was tunnel-visioned on the beast, but could sense that there were many humans nearby. Either they had listened to Michael and Minerva, or they hadn't. No matter what though, Alana had a job to do.

She wrapped her arms around the beast and removed her from Michael, whirling and dragging her. The humans watched in awe as Alana grabbed the beast by the throat and raised her into the air. The beast choked and gasped, wearing the face of a beautiful woman who was, in all reality, so rotten on the inside.

"Say it," Alana demanded, her voice dripping with pure hatred. "Tell the humans what you've done."

The feeling of rage swirled within Alana, but it was under control. The hyper-focus chewed away at her incessant gnawing hunger for blood, at least for now. In that moment, the world just consisted of Alana and the beast.

Choking and gagging, the enemy vampire eventually caught her breath as Alana loosened her grip just a little. She sank her claws into Alana's wrist and her lips twisted into a cruel grin. Then, she began to laugh.

"They call me The Beast of Temes. The trophies I collect are a testament to my territory, my glory, and *your* reality. Mankind will always be prey to the vampire. Your charade here? A false mask. Even if I fall tonight, it will be known that deep down, in the pit of your soul, you are exactly the same as I am."

"WHY?!" Alana screamed.

She slammed the bitter vampire into the tree again and again. The beast coughed up blood, shuddering from the impact. And yet, despite this, she still continued to laugh through it all.

"Why? It is in our nature. That other vampire spoke your name. Alana, is it? I told you. I show the beauty in death, and I show reality. You can question me on this many times over, and the answer will not change," the beast purred.

Crying out in fury, Alana turned to look over her shoulder. Michael had dragged himself over to Minerva's daughter. The woman's wounds were severe. Minerva could do nothing but crouch down helplessly, her hand over her heart. The villagers observed, motionless and powerless to what was going on. No one had thought to bring medical equipment, an oversight that could be paid for dearly.

Alana zeroed in on the thumping of a heart. *Minerva's daughter… I can hear it. It's… getting slower.*

Lubdub..lubdub…lubdub…..lub….dub…

Soft, pained cries emitted from Minerva, filling Alana's entire being. Muffled laughter sounded out around her other senses. The beast – she found this all amusing.

"Aww, couldn't save my prey? What a shame. Now, maybe, reality will…"

Alana didn't want to hear it. She charged her fangs into the throat of the enemy vampire and dug right into her flesh. A sickening squelching noise could be heard as Alana plucked the threads of life from her enemy, blood coating her clothing, her skin, and her hair.

The beast wearing beauty's face clung to life – just barely – as Alana turned to one of the pikes. With her free hand, she grabbed the bottom of the displayed skeleton and tugged, ripping it off and down from the metal. With the neck of her enemy still in one hand, she crouched and launched herself towards the top of the pike. With all of her strength, Alana lifted the beast and punctured her torso on the spike.

Screaming out in sheer agony and thrashing about, the evil vampire moaned and whimpered as the last bits of life dripped down the pike, adding to the stains of the victims impaled upon it previously.

A colony of bats flew above, screeching hauntingly. Victory was claimed by Alana, but only after so much loss.

Chapter Nine

T he silence of the night was unbearable. Tears poured down Minerva's face as she held the corpse of her daughter, bringing her close and burying her face into the body. Blood was smeared all over the grieving woman, and she shook with sobs, sniffling loudly.

"I'm so sorry that I wasn't there for you, my love. I am so sorry," she cried.

Alana, covered in blood from the beast, closed her eyes, allowing tears to slowly glide down her cheeks. She had promised Minerva so many times that they would find her daughter alive. It hurt so badly to know that she'd failed. All the same, Minerva needed her now. The townsfolk remained in a state of shock as the vampire approached her friend.

She crouched down to be close to Minerva, gently placing a hand on her shoulder. Minerva lifted her head from the body, taking in a deep breath. More tears spilled from her eyes.

"We planned on exploring the world together," she said in a pained voice. "She was so stressed about the loss of her father to that ailment, and I was hurting so much as well. We wanted to get out of our hometown and just… start anew. I thought we were going to be ok. She was my everything. She cannot leave now. There must be something we can do."

The inevitability of death was on full display. Alana didn't want to mislead Minerva.

"She would have been so proud of you here, Minerva," the vampire whispered softly. "She has moved on, and is looking down upon us, if that is what you believe."

Minerva's eyes fell upon the limp body of her daughter. She drew her hand along her cheek, shuddering suddenly, and clenching her fist.

"You can turn her. Correct?" she pleaded to Alana. "Please, do it now."

"That is not how it works," Alana replied, wincing. "Plus, I would not want to turn anyone unwillingly. Minerva, I was born this way. I cannot imagine how a human would feel having to be like this."

Minerva shouted out in pure fury.

Michael wandered over. Defeated, Minerva didn't bother begging him. He merely bowed his head, allowing some of his hair to fall into his face. Several tears made their way down his cheeks as well, resting on his sharp jawline and gently dripping off.

The townsfolk whispered amongst themselves once more, entirely unsure as to what they could do. The consensus was, no doubt, to leave things be until the grieving mother could come to terms with her daughter's death.

As she continued to cry over the limp body of her daughter, Minerva's anger subsided a little, her muscles relaxing.

"I'm sorry for being so demanding of you," she whimpered to Alana in a muffled voice. "I just… I cannot bear to lose her…"

"It's alright," Alana said, her tone firm, but kind.

Hesitantly, the townsfolk closed in, causing the vampire to give a low growl. The man who had splashed Alana and Michael with the holy water bowed his head and cleared his throat.

"Our initial reactions were unfounded," he said. "We realise that now. You destroyed the real beast. Please, how can we be of assistance?"

Alana studied the man while still trying to soothe her friend who was dealing with immense loss.

"We need to honour the dead," the vampire said, heartbroken. "Please, help me in preparing graves for those who have fallen. Every last skeleton here deserves to have a decent burial."

The man looked towards the impaled skeletons and shuddered. He ran a charcoal-stained hand through his hair, clearly uncomfortable from the entire ordeal.

"What about the pikes?" he asked.

"They should stay here as a reminder of what happened," Minerva spoke up, still shaky and dripping with despair. "They should be changed into something different though. We will figure something out. For now… we will honour the fallen."

Alana cast a curious glance to Minerva. The woman looked incredibly determined.

Chapter Ten

By the next dusk, the skeletons were dismantled, properly buried, and given their own marks. Minerva, Michael and Alana stood by the open casket of the human woman's deceased daughter as more tears were shed. Minerva stared up to the sky, furrowing her brow.

"Please," she whispered into the wind. "Whoever might be up there, bring her back to me. Or, if she is there, treat her well."

The flutter of wings alerted Alana to a colony of bats. She caught her breath as a few of them landed beneath the branches nearby, hanging upside down. Her nostrils flared but her muscles relaxed as soon as only the musk of bat hit her senses; there was no indication of human or vampire blood.

As if having read Alana's mind, Michael spoke up.

"There are no signs of others here, Alana," he said with confidence. "In fact, I will be leaving soon. My work here is done. But before I leave, I will educate you on what I know. After we've honoured the fallen, of course."

Managing a sad smile, Alana nodded, closing her eyes and bowing her head. She would hate to turn out like the beast. Although she had done an excellent job of controlling her urges so far, that gnawing feeling was ever-present.

As she observed Minerva's every whimper and cry, Alana's bloodlust was mercifully silent. Despite the pang of grief in her gut though, she knew it would return.

"Remember the time we came upon several old statues, when you were really young, and we played hide-and-seek?" the human woman whispered, as if talking to her daughter's spirit. "You looked upon those pieces of history with such wonder. I knew right then that you would be just like me. A mother suffers the loss of her daughter tonight. Why is the world so cruel? If only we had…"

As a choked sob billowed out from the woman's chest, Alana placed a hand upon her shoulder, stopping her in mid-sentence.

"The "what ifs" will only torture you, Minerva. There is nothing, truly, that could have been done. The beast was relentless. From the way she spoke, I knew there was pure evil in the pit of her soul. There was nothing that you, I, or Michael could have done differently. I am so sorry for your loss, my friend."

Minerva stared at the casket. Dark as midnight, it had little red roses painted on the cover here and there. Finally, she bowed her head and lapsed into silence, realising that Alana was right.

"I wish to be alone with her," Minerva muttered. "I will catch up with you at your home – and get some rest – later. But, for now, I need some space."

"Of course," Alana replied.

The two vampires left Minerva to grieve, knowing that there wouldn't be any more beasts nearby.

As they walked through the town, they received passing, curious looks. It made Alana feel self-conscious. She glanced over to Michael for reassurance.

"What of this place now?" she asked. "They know of us. Are you worried that they might try and purge us?"

Michael shrugged, his gaze landing upon several villagers as he gave a nod in greeting to them. They were hesitant, but they had seen how he and Alana had faced off against the beast. That, and his attempt to save Minerva's daughter.

"No," he said after a long pause. "I hold no such worry. If they wanted to make an attempt to kill us, they would have done so by now. However, it might be best for me to leave soon. As a matter of fact, they might consider *you* a hero, after your display. I am unconcerned. Word travels, but it will be framed as urban legend, just like the beast. This has happened before in many towns, and despite our secret being a loose one, myth and rumour will become dominant again over time."

Alana nodded, accepting Michael's answer. She felt a pang of sadness at the thought of him leaving.

"But what of your teachings?" she asked. "I have so much to learn, and clearly you are more knowledgeable than I am. That gnawing… I don't want to be a monster."

"You have proven that you are far from it, Alana," Michael replied.

They walked down the street, the scent of baked goods wafting through the air having no effect on them. The beating hearts and adrenaline of the townsfolk, however, did. Alana, at least, was able to ignore that for now.

"Before I depart," Michael said. "I will give you more insight into how our world works now. I think you will be at peace then – at least, for the most part."

Accepting his answer, Alana led Michael to her home for one last time. Although her mind was racing with so many thoughts, she remembered to do a detour to pick something up for Minerva. She would give it to the woman later.

Chapter Eleven

Entering Alana's house, the vampires took a seat at the table where they had first dined on blood together. Alana endeavoured to ignore the stains she had left there. Instead, she studied Michael. His shoulders were slumped and he had dark rings under his eyes. He returned Alana's stare, the murky depths of his deep brown gaze swirling with grief. The crimson had faded, for now, at least.

A pause that felt like hours – but was really only a few seconds – grew. The male vampire broke it with a heavy sigh.

"Minerva is concerned that she did not do enough back there, but I feel the same," he said. "I had heard about the problems in Temes and I wanted to help. Despite dedicating myself to helping the humans, one died under my watch. She'd lost so much blood."

"Please don't blame yourself," Alana said.

She reached out to take his hand. He flinched in surprise, but relaxed moments after. Studying her expression, he soon nodded.

"I must bear that in mind," he said. "After everything I've experienced in my relatively long life, some things can still be incredibly painful. It is certainly a myth that feelings fade over time. My propensity to feel raw emotion is just as strong as it was long ago. I wonder if it's different for every vampire."

Deep in thought, his gaze seemed distant until he noticed that he had Alana's full attention. Snapping out of his reverie, he glanced at the blood stains on the table.

"Anyway," he said. "You wanted to know about my use of donors. Correct?"

Alana nodded keenly, an almost pleading desperation in her eyes.

"Some humans know all about vampires and seek to help us," Michael explained. "They offer their blood, and in exchange, we offer them knowledge and protection. My service is to humankind; those who work in a symbiotic relationship with us. I was sent here to be of aid, and whilst I haven't succeeded to contribute as much as I wanted to, meeting you and being able to help you with your inner turmoil has certainly been positive."

"Well," said Alana. "You've helped more than you know. The townsfolk saw you and I working together. Not only that, but I was cornered there by the beast. If you hadn't jumped in to help me, I don't know if I would have won. Give yourself more credit."

"Fair point," Michael said, nodding in acknowledgement. "I have a map and addresses of donors close by and within your town here. I suggest that you contact them. Alana, after your heroic deeds, I feel certain that you will bring even more positive change to this world than you already have. You do not have to live with that gnawing hunger. There are other ways to combat that bloodlust – and you have what it takes, my friend. Anyway, my work here is done. I have much to look into, and while I wish I could stay and help this town mend, that will now fall on your shoulders. I am sorry."

Alana frowned deeply, looking down at her

fingers and tapping them upon the table. She closed her eyes for just a moment, feeling a pang of sadness. Though they hadn't known each other for very long, she felt a connection with Michael. This friendship was important; he had opened up the world to her, and had inspired her to see the *good* side of her kind.

"Will we meet again?" she asked hopefully.

Michael stood up and gently patted her on the shoulder. Then, when he turned towards the door, all Alana could do was watch.

"Perhaps," he said, an endearing honesty in his tone. "I look forward to hearing of your great deeds if we do meet again sometime later down the line. Goodbye, Alana. And I wish you the very best with your future journeys. Keep that spark of life, will you?"

"I will," Alana replied. "And don't lose your love for the small animals that you adore so much."

Alana's sweetness prompted a chuckle from the gentleman vampire. With that, he exited Alana's house, vanishing into the night. The flapping of bat wings could be heard as he flew towards the moon. He was off to hunt other beasts.

Alana wandered through the house, rubbing her temples and trying to take everything in. Her muscles screamed at her from exhaustion, protesting the fact that she was still up and moving. Not having yet rested after that battle with the beast, she realised that she had no option but to allow herself to recuperate. The gnawing hunger was like a fly buzzing around her head. For now though, she managed to ignore it.

She wanted to collapse into her soft sheets, but let out a groan, knowing that other things needed to be done. First, she crawled into the bathroom and turned on the shower to the hottest setting. Once ready, she entered, taking notice of the river of crimson flowing down her flesh as she washed herself off. Her many wounds stung, reminding her that she would need several days of rest soon. With the beast dead, and the town safe, she decided that it would be alright to take some time out for self-care.

Finding herself a black nightgown, she noticed the mess of sheets on her bed. She longingly stared for a moment before wandering into the living room once more. The detour on her way back with Michael had allowed her to pick up some more stew for Minerva. She wasn't sure when the lady would be back, but hoped that she would avoid an inn and stay here again.

Alana's worries dissipated when, upon hearing a knock at the door, a familiar scent wafted towards her.

"Come in," she called out.

As Minerva walked in, her cheeks were clearly tear-stained. Her shoulders were slumped and her mousy brown hair had several strands messily hanging in her face. Her scent was that of dirt and sorrow.

Her joints creaked as she made her way to the couch, collapsing down beside Alana and letting out a choked sigh. She buried her face into her hands and tried to cry, but the tears wouldn't come. In that moment, she had none left to shed. She had nothing left but the pit of ever-swirling sorrow in her stomach.

"I got you some more stew and bread," Alana said softly. "I can leave you be, if you wish. But if you need to talk, I'm here. Really."

Minerva didn't respond for a few moments, but then lifted her head from her hands.

"Thank you for your kindness, Alana. This is just so difficult. I feel an overbearing sense of darkness. My body feels numb, as does my brain. The future seems so bleak."

"Well," Alana said. "I know that I say I don't like to focus on the past. But... sometimes, at the right times, it can be a positive thing. Comforting. Why don't you tell me about the good times you and your daughter had? Let's honour her memory together."

After a pause, Minerva nodded. A small smile played on her lips as she began to delve into stories of exploration and wonder – all that they'd seen together on their travels. At some point, she was even able to give a bittersweet laugh, touching her forehead in slight disbelief at the action. The tears did return, every so often, gliding down her cheeks. But with Alana by her side and listening to her memories – keeping them alive – well, maybe things would be alright.

Chapter Twelve

For several weeks after her daughter's passing did Minerva remain in the town. With Alana, she visited her daughter's grave every day, placing a rose by the tombstone every time. Although Minerva worked hard to think back to happier times, there were countless moments where, understandably, she broke down. Alana was always there for her throughout. The support enabled Minerva to accept the harsh reality that her daughter was gone forever.

The townsfolk were wary around Alana, but also rather curious. The vampire received several questions, some even regarding Michael and his whereabouts. She didn't have to deal with any more angry mobs, thankfully, but knew the time would soon be right to move on.

Winter was just around the corner, and the solstice was being celebrated to honour the lost.

Dewdrops turned to frost, something abundantly clear as Alana wandered through the woods. Crouching down towards a rose bush, being careful of the thorns, she picked a flower. She examined the sparkling ivory frost on the petals, giving a smile at the bittersweet beauty. Many plants would wither and die now, but would return again in the spring. Death was horrible, but it could be beautiful as well. Alana was determined to refuse a grisly, horrible death to innocent humans.

Soon, she arrived at her destination: the pikes that had held skeletons as trophies from the beast just weeks ago. They were now cleaned of blood, their metal shining in the final rays of the setting sun. Alana was thankful that the rays were subtle; they made it possible for her to stand in the last gaze of the sun as day lapsed into night. She had always found the sunsets to be too beautiful to miss.

The vampire's gaze set upon the pikes, which were adorned with two peculiar additions. Bat houses and bird houses were attached rather sturdily upon the instruments that had previously been used for death. Now, they would house new life; an appropriate and tasteful turn for an otherwise horrible event.

Alana smiled, noticing several birds that wouldn't migrate for the winter as they gathered up sticks and other ground debris for their nests. She was so lost in her observations that she jumped when she sensed someone walking up behind her. She quickly spun around and was relieved to see that it was Minerva, who was in a dark blouse and leggings of the same colour. The middle-aged woman gave a light nod.

"Hello there, dear. Sorry to startle you," Minerva said in a heavy tone.

Ever since the incident, her voice was always tinged in sadness. Alana couldn't blame her for that, not one bit.

"It's alright, Minerva. There's no need to apologise. Thank you for meeting me here. How are you feeling today?" Alana questioned, concern evident in her voice.

"Just ok," Minerva sighed. "I think I will be feeling like this for a while. I have accepted reality. But the pain will never fade away. My love for my daughter was so strong; we had a close relationship. Now is not the time to dwell on that though. You wanted to speak with me, Alana?"

"Yes," Alana muttered, somewhat hesitantly. "I will be leaving Temes very soon. There is so much for me to do in this world, and I've decided that it's time to move on. I wanted to ask you if you'd like to come with me."

Although she was relieved to have told Minerva the news, the feeling of having voiced it aloud weighed heavily on Alana's heart. An overbearing silence hung in the air, the breeze much colder now as it blistered through their thick clothing. The chiming of birds did nothing to reduce the tension. Rather than a feeling made from anger though, it was one of sorrow. Alana already had a sense of what Minerva's answer was going to be. It caused her to wince and brace herself.

"Thank you, dear," Minerva said, smiling gratefully. "But the answer is, unfortunately, no. I do not have the spirit to travel. Not right now. Maybe one day. This does not have to be goodbye forever though. Right? You will at least visit Temes?"

As Minerva wiped away a stray tear, Alana was keen to reassure her.

"Of course I will," Alana confirmed. "In that

case, I would love it if you'd accept my offer of staying at my house. It needs to be cared for by someone with a positive energy – something that I know you have in abundance. You may not feel that way at the moment of course, but I know, deep down, that you are strong."

"Oh Alana, I could not…"

"I insist," Alana cut in. "You have helped me through my own inner demons, Minerva, and I am forever grateful for that. You, and Michael, have taught me that I should not hate myself; that I can *be me* without having to wallow in the corners of my mind. I found it so hard to accept myself before. Please. You have been living in that house now since the day we met. It's the least I can do."

Biting her lip, Minerva nodded, closing her eyes for a moment.

"Could I give you a hug, dear?" the woman asked finally.

At Alana's nod, Minerva gently walked over, appreciatively wrapping her arms around her.

"You remind me of someone," Minerva

whispered into Alana's ear. "I could never quite put my finger on it before. But yes, I understand now. You remind me of my daughter. You have the same spirit within you that she had. And I know you will do good by this world. Keep that spark, Alana."

A tear crawled down Alana's cheek, and she gave a genuine, bright smile. Her expression lit up the night, and the stars seemed to return her smile with their vibrant shine as the rays from the sun faded into dusk entirely.

"That is a huge honour, Minerva. Thank you so much," Alana finally said.

The two strong friends observed the stars together, discussing the bird and bat houses for a little while. The crisp of winter reminded them that it was time to head home. They left for the house, soon to be Minerva's, a little while later.

The atmosphere in Temes was much warmer than it had been out in the woods. Blazing fires danced in select pits, out of the way of the road.

Alana walked past a few, warming her hands and exchanging kind words with some of the townsfolk. A few walked up to her with questions aplenty: "Rumour has it that you're leaving. So soon? It will be a shame for Temes to lose a hero."

Confirming the facts, much to their dismay, Alana reassured the townsfolk that one day, she would be back.

The newspapers had refrained from mentioning anything about vampire attacks. The town had decided to keep it as their little secret. Truthfully, it was doubtful that the outside world would believe in such folklore anyway. Rather, the tale of the beast's defeat was painted as the story of a serial killer who had finally been brought to justice, which really, wasn't too far from the truth.

There was still the matter of Alana's bloodlust, and her need to satiate it. Michael had not been wrong. Soon after he'd left, she had investigated the locations he had informed her of, finding the donors herself. When she had explained the situation to them, they were sympathetic and understanding. "You don't have to kill to feed," they had told her. "We can cover your needs. You are the beast slayer? Especially so, due to that. Thank you so much for saving our town."

At first, Alana had been overwhelmed and was worried that she would take too much blood without even realising it. Minerva had taught her many things though, and one of them was control. That night when Minerva had begged Alana to stop had signified something that the vampire needed tremendously; the reassurance that she *could* stop drinking if she needed to.

With that, she had a mechanism of control, and ever so slowly, that gnawing was tamed. Prior to finalising the house situation with Minerva, she stopped by for a drink of the delicious crimson liquid, profusely thanking the donor. Her hunger – along with the need to feed from the source – satisfied, Alana returned home for her last goodbyes.

Another hug was exchanged between Alana and Minerva. The human woman cupped Alana's cheek after pulling away, giving a smile.

"Never forget, Alana. I am so proud of you. This whole town is. I will be heartbroken for a long while. But you have helped me to see the light again and empowered me to get through some terrible times. You stayed with me all night when I broke down crying. You were there to listen to my many, many stories. Even beyond just taking down my daughter's killer, you have heart, and you have spirit. Thank you."

"I am honoured, Minerva. Stay strong, alright? Much of the reason I'm alright now is because of you. I will never forget *that* either. See you soon, my friend. I promise to visit when I can."

The goodbye was as bittersweet as the looming frost of the season. Alana picked up her cloak, pulled her hood up, and wandered out into the night. The future didn't look bleak anymore now that she had control of her bloodlust. That burning self-hatred had dissipated, and with a confident feeling, she had a new purpose.

Her warm brown eyes sparkled as she walked towards the stars, a new objective in mind. No more hiding, no more hating. She knew the feeling of being locked down by bloodlust. She'd seen the result of vampires that had abandoned all empathy, leaving their past selves for dead, a hollow shell. Now, she knew that she wasn't among vampires like that, and that most importantly, she wouldn't turn into one either.

A smile spread across her face as she looked to the moon, the cold wind not so cold anymore. Across the moon flew a colony of bats, something she was certainly familiar with. Now, it was time to join them.

Taking in a deep breath, the frigid air caressing her lungs, she allowed her form to melt away and shift into a bat. Unlike last time, she could fly correctly. Her emotions were no longer limiting her true ability.

After all this time, her bloodlust was silent, and her mind was free. She flew off into the night, towards the stars, to help other vampires like her and to fight other beasts. From her claws hung a little bag with several of her favourite books.

Alana was finally at peace with herself.

****